WORKSONG

WORKSONG

WRITTEN BY

Gary Paulsen

ILLUSTRATED BY

Ruth Wright Paulsen

Voyager Books
Harcourt, Inc.
SAN DIEGO   NEW YORK   LONDON

For information about permission to reproduce selections from this book,
write to trade.permissions@hmhco.com or to Permissions, Houghton Mifflin
Harcourt Publishing Company, 3 Park Avenue, 19th Floor, New York, New York 10016.

First Voyager Books edition 2000
Voyager Books is a registered trademark of Harcourt, Inc.

The Library of Congress has cataloged the hardcover edition as follows:
Paulsen, Gary.
Worksong/written by Gary Paulsen; illustrated by Ruth Wright Paulsen.
p.   cm.
Summary: Illustrations and rhyming text depict people doing all kinds of work.
[1. Occupations—Fiction.   2. Stories in rhyme.] I. Paulsen, Ruth Wright, ill.   II. Title.
PZ8.3.27369Wo   1997
[E]—dc20   95-49309
ISBN 0-15-200980-9
ISBN 0-15-202371-2 pb

LEO 20 19 18 17
4500682882

Printed in China

This book is dedicated
with all admiration and respect
to Nancy Flannery

It is keening noise and jolting sights,

and hammers flashing in the light,

and houses up and
trees in sun,

and trucks on one more nighttime run.

It is fresh new food to fill the plates,

and flat, clean sidewalks to try to skate,
and towering buildings that were not there,
hanging suddenly in the air.

It is offices filled with glowing screens

and workers making steel beams,

and ice-cream cones to lick and wear,

and all the pins that
hold your hair.

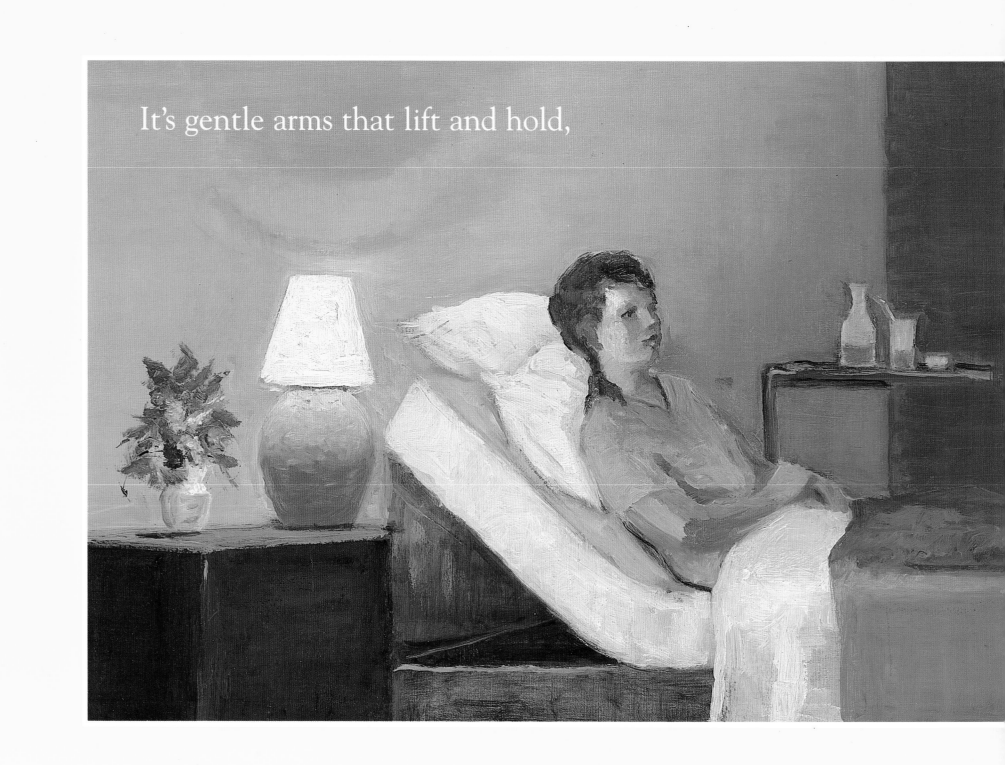

It's gentle arms that lift and hold,

and all the soldiers
brave and bold,

and help to fit the brand-new shoes,

and hands to show you books to use.

It is people here and
people there, making
things for all to share;

all the things there are to be,
and nearly all there is to see.